Cheetah, Bulls and Snails

'OK, listen up class. I have a special announcement to make. We are going to have a competition!' Ms Books announced.

I sat up straighter. I love Maths competitions. Last year I won the Sudoku competition and got the "Maths Wizard" badge.

I raised my hand.

'Yes, Arjun?'

'Is it a Maths competition?' I crossed my sweaty fingers, hoping this would be the case.

HUNGRY TO READ

Arti Sonthalia

Illustrations
Sumedha Saha

SCHOLASTIC
New York Toronto London Auckland
Sydney New Delhi Hong Kong

Dedicated to the
Lotus Feet of My Guru.

Published by Scholastic India Pvt. Ltd.
A subsidiary of Scholastic Inc., New York, 10012 (USA).
Publishers since 1920, with international operations in Canada, Australia, New Zealand, the United Kingdom, India, and Hong Kong.

For information regarding permission, write to:
Scholastic India Pvt. Ltd.
A-27, Ground Floor, Sigma Centre
Infocity-1, Sector 34, Gurgaon 122001 (India)

First edition: August 2017
Reprint April 2019, January 2022

ISBN-13: 978-93-5275-174-7

Printed at Ram Printograph, Delhi

Contents

From the other end of the room, Sheen butted in, 'Ms Books, I am so thrilled! Please tell us about the competition.' She raised her chin so high that it could touch the ceiling.

'It's a *Read Drive*,' Ms Books said excitedly.

'*Read Drive*!' everyone gasped. Even Rehan, the distracted kid, who never paid attention to anything, stared at Ms Books.

I looked at Tejas, my best friend. Tejas was playing with his red lucky pencil. He did this every time he was delighted and nervous.

Last year when Tejas had won the Spelling Bee competition, he had used that pencil, and since then, he always kept it with him as his lucky charm.

'*Read Drive* is a reading competition between 3A and 3B. The section that wins the competition gets ...' Ms Books waited.

'Wow ... a reading competition!' Tejas yelled as

though he had just woken up to the news, and this competition was the best thing in the world. He kissed his red lucky pencil and beamed.

'A *Read Drive*?' I asked disgustedly. Did something like this exist? Or was it all Ms Books' idea? I wondered, because she loved books. No one even knew her original name! We all called her Ms Books because she was always reading.

And I *hated* reading!

'*What gets the class?*' Rio, the talkative girl who spoke bad English, asked.

'What does the class get?' Sheen corrected her.

'The class gets to do a night stay in school, and since we are starting with the solar system unit in class, we all get to see the planetary system through a telescope!' Ms Books nearly fell off her seat with excitement.

'Yay!' Everyone screamed and jumped up and down.

A night stay in school without parental supervision! And seeing through a real telescope! Now this was something thrilling! I had never done this before.

Tejas did a high five with me.

I suddenly realised we would have to read in order to stay a night in school and see through the telescope. This was like the worst mathematical equation ever.

Rio raised her hand again. '*But how win* Read Drive *from 3B*?' she asked.

Sheen looked angrily at Rio for always speaking wrong English, and corrected her again. 'How can we win this *Read Drive* from 3B?'

I quickly did the calculation in my mind. 3B had seven Cheetah readers (the fast readers), five Bull readers (the moderate speed readers, fighting their way up to the Cheetah) and three Snail readers, the slooowwwwest.

As for our section, we had five Cheetah readers, five Bull readers and five Snail readers, and the worst part of it all was that I was one of the Snail readers!

I had been a Snail from Grade 1, along with the distracted kid, Rehan.

'But Ms Books, I have already done the calculation—our section is going to lose; 3B has better readers than us,' I said sadly.

'Your calculation is good, Arjun, but we do have some fine readers in our class too.' She looked at Tejas, Sheen and the other Cheetah readers.

'How are we going to decide what kind of books are going to be counted? Tejas asked. 'I mean, I could read a million easy books a day.'

'*Are you count easy books with picture on each page?*' Rio asked.

Sheen was about to correct Rio when Ms Books said, 'You decide according to the group you are in. If you are in the Cheetah group, you read the longer chapter books, if you are in the Bull group, you read the shorter chapter books with fewer pictures, and if you are in the Snail group,' Ms Books looked at me, 'you read the books with pictures on most pages and very few words.'

'*But who check what we read?*' Rio went on with her questions.

Sheen annoyingly stomped her foot, looking at Rio.

Ms Books said, 'Every morning when you come in, you write the names of the books you have read on the white tally sheet I have hung on the wall in front of the class. If I think the book is not of your level, I will not count it. More importantly, I trust you all.'

'So, two weeks from now, Friday evening we are going to total the number of books read by both 3A and 3B. Then, whichever section wins will get to take part in the night stay on Saturday and see through the telescope!' Ms Books said.

Reading?

'Now, class, we can all go to the library and choose some books, so that you can help your class win the competition,' Ms Books said.

Rio and Sheen both raised their hands, but this time Sheen didn't wait for Rio to talk. 'Ms Books, will there be an award for the best reader?'

'Oh yes, yes, the best reader gets a special golden badge to wear to school every day.'

I looked at Tejas as he waved his lucky pencil

harder and I knew he would read all the books in the world to win this competition.

'Arjun and all the Snail readers, I can help you choose some books from the library that you can take home during the weekend.' Ms Books smiled as if this was going to be the best weekend ever.

I had planned on playing a superhero game with Tejas on the computer, but I was sure that after the golden badge announcement, Tejas would not be interested in anything but *reading!*

'You can try reading some simple biographies—they are interesting to read,' Ms Books announced.

'What's a biography?' Sheen asked.

'It's a true story about a person's life,' Tejas said.

Ms Books smiled. 'Yes, it has to be a famous person, someone like Gandhi.'

'Who is Gandhi?' Rio asked.

'Mahatma Gandhi was a leader who helped

Drive

India get its independence through non-violence,' Ms Books said.

'What's non-violence?' Sheen asked.

'Non-violence is the use of peaceful means to bring about change. Gandhi was unique in his ways. He fought for freedom but he loved even those he fought.'

I raised my hand and asked softly, 'What about kids who don't like reading and still want to participate in the night stay and see through the telescope?'

This time I had caught Rehan's attention.

Ms Books smiled. 'I understand, Arjun. You would love to see through the telescope, but all you need to do is put in a little effort, and that way you could help your class win.'

I didn't think it was going to be a "little" effort. It was going to be a *whole* lot of effort. Ms Books had really given us a book challenge for the night stay in school and seeing through the telescope. This was too good an opportunity to miss!

'*Ms Books, happens what to losing class?*' Rio inquired. She sometimes speaks uncannily like Yoda from *Star Wars* actually.

'Yes, Rio, since everyone is going to put in some effort, it would be fair to have ice cream cones for the losing class too,' Ms Books replied kindly.

'At least we would get the ice cream cones, because we were no match to the 3B Cheetah readers,' I thought.

Rehan gave a big sigh of relief.

We were all headed to the library.

'Hey Arjun, who do you think will get the golden badge?' Tejas asked enthusiastically.

'Of course, you! Mathematically speaking, you are the fastest reader in our class, even better than Sheen, though she is not far behind.'

Tejas smiled and made swift motions with his lucky pencil. 'Arjun, you are the best mathematician in the world.' We did another high five.

'But ... in 3B there is a fast Cheetah reader, Annika, and she is fast, really fast, maybe faster than you.'

Tejas looked nervous now. 'How do you know that, Arjun?'

'Well, a mathematician knows everything,' I said proudly.

'Oh, come on, tell me, tell me, tell me ...' Tejas coaxed in his usual tone.

'Kyra, my little monstrous sister, and Annika's sister, Ambi, are the besssst of friends—they share everything. I mean *everything*! Kyra even knows the names of the books the Cheetah reader Annika reads,' I said.

'So what?' Tejas asked.

'So, she can read one of your "all words" books with no pictures very very quickly.'

Tejas chewed on his lucky pencil.

'Annika's house, room, bathroom, closet and even bathtub are full of books.' I could have mentioned the toilet, the fridge and the oven. But I didn't want to scare Tejas—after all, he was my best friend.

But Tejas already seemed super worried.

'Don't worry, I am sure you can beat her.' I tried to fire him up.

Tejas looked as if butterflies were nibbling at his stomach. 'How many books are you taking home, Arjun?'

'You know I don't like reading.' I gave Tejas an angry look.

'But it's a competition, and our class will lose if you don't read, and we will never be part of the night stay!' He was right. No win, no night stay, and no seeing through a telescope!

'I hate story-books. They are so made up!' I groaned.

'But a book is your ... *like* your best friend,' Tejas said.

'You are comparing me with your story-books!' I snapped at Tejas.

How could Tejas ever compare me to his dead books, which were so unrealistic and contained all made-up stuff from some author whose brains were stuffed with useless words?

How boring!

I was not going to let any words fill up my mind because my mind was already filled with numbers, and to me, Maths was very interesting. Not boring like books!

The Race

We reached the library, and in the library we couldn't talk, because someone had the brilliant insight that reading was best done in silence! So Tejas and I took some time off from each other.

I settled down with a Sudoku puzzle on the comfy couch while distracted Rehan busily played with his toy dinosaur. Rehan loved dinosaurs.

Rio was still searching for the right book to read while Sheen had already started reading. Tejas had so many books in his hands that all I could see of his face was the tip of his nose.

I wondered if he thought the end of the world was close, and he wouldn't get another chance to read.

He really was a reading wizard!

I spotted Annika, the 3B Cheetah reader. She had

piles and piles of books next to her. If she read at this rate, 3B was sure to win the night stay, and we would have to settle for ice cream.

I decided the best thing for me to do was complete my Sudoku puzzle.

After finishing my Sudoku, I whispered to Rehan, 'Hey, do you want to read?'

'No,' he said.

'Don't like reading?'

'No.'

'Why?' I asked.

'Boring,' he said.

'Lets play!' he offered.

I smiled and was glad at least someone else shared my opinion.

I was about to tell Rehan about the new number game that Mom had taught me, when Ms Books whispered, 'Arjun and Rehan, I don't see any books with you. Don't you want to help your class win?'

She took out two books from the shelf.

She gave Rehan the first one. 'If you read this with me, you'll have one book to your name to begin with.'

Rehan looked at the words on the page and then at Ms Books. He did that again and again and again.

'Read, Rehan.' She tried to encourage him.

Rehan stared at the shelves, his eyes moving back and forth across the rows of books, and whispered, 'Boring!'

'No, Rehan, reading is not boring, it makes you a thinker,' Ms Books whispered.

But Rehan was already thinking a lot about dinosaurs. And if he thought any more, his mind would explode. So, if reading really made you think, then it was the worst choice to make!

Ms Books turned to look at me. 'Arjun, could you please read this book for me?'

I looked at the book. It was a reader, *Level Two—Knights and Fairies*. And before she could say anything, I said, 'Ms Books, I don't like reading about knights or fairies—they are not real.'

She gave me a forced smile. 'That's OK, Arjun, we could read about something that's real. How about this one?' she took out another book.

It was named *Spiders' Lunch*.

I screeched, 'Eeks! I hate spiders!'

'Shhhhh ... OK, how about this one, *Princess Buttercups?*

'Too girlie,' I said.

'This one?' she asked.

'Looks too sad. I'll cry.'

'This one?'

'Too kiddish.'

'This one?'

'I hate robots.'

'This one?'

'Too scary.'

She sighed.

'See, Ms Books, there is no book in the world

that's made for me.' I wondered why I felt sad when I said that.

Ms Books looked into my eyes. 'Some famous man once said, *There is a book for everyone.* You just haven't found it yet, Arjun. Maybe by the end of the *Read Drive* you will find it.' With that she left and didn't ask me to carry a book home.

I quickly ran to pick up my younger sister Kyra from her class.

Drama Queen

A smart girl like Kyra didn't need assistance to walk from Grade One to the bus, *but* my little sister made me walk with her to the bus every day!

'Can we walk a little faster so that I can sit with Tejas in the bus?' I asked, feeling annoyed.

Tejas had refused to walk with Kyra. He had laughed, 'It's a girlie thing to walk with your sister.' From that day onwards, all the fun of running to the bus with Tejas had stopped.

'But aren't you going to sit with me in the bus?' Kyra stamped her foot and stood still.

'Why do I have to sit with you every time? Why can't I sit with my friends?' I asked.

Kyra's lower lip began to pout, her eyes welled up with crocodile tears and her bag fell on the ground.

The drama began. If she stuck her lip out any further, a bird could sit on it.

Before her whining started, I quickly picked up her bag and lowered my voice. 'OK! I will sit with you, drama queen!'

She didn't budge. 'I am going to tell Mom you called me drama queen,' she threatened. Her lips drooped further.

Now the second part of the drama: The Mummy Blackmail.

'OK, Kyra,' I did my best to sound sorry. 'I shall sit with you.' Ms Books was right—maybe Gandhi's non-violence worked even with your little sister.

She immediately smiled and we ran to the bus together.

I attempted to sneak out to where Tejas, Rehan and Rio were sitting. 'If you don't sit with me, I will tell Mom,' she said.

What a bully! Younger siblings always had the advantage of the *"I-am-going-to-tell-Mom"* weapon.

My calculation told me I would have to put up with Kyra for thirteen full minutes till we reached our stop, unless someone came to my rescue.

Tejas soon came up to my seat. 'Arjun, how many books did you borrow from the library to help our class win the reading competition?'

And before I opened my mouth to tell Tejas, 'None', Kyra jumped in, saying, 'Wow ... a reading competition!' as if the competition was for her. What a pain she was!

'I am going to read more books than all of you put together, and win this competition!' she announced.

'But it's not for your grade!' I stopped her before she made more plans.

'Yes, Kyra, it's only for third graders, and the best part is,' Tejas went on excitedly, 'the class that wins gets to have a night stay in school and see through a telescope!'

'Not fair! Third graders get to do everything.' She crossed her arms in front of her and slouched down in her seat.

'And guess what! The best reader gets a golden badge, which he can wear to school everyday!' Tejas was so thrilled about the badge and the reading competition, I wondered how heartbroken he would be if he didn't win this.

'A golden badge! I wish I was a third grader, then I could win the golden badge,' Kyra said.

'But you are not a third grader!' I clenched my teeth.

Kyra's face fell again.

Tejas knew what a drama queen she was. 'Kyra, I am sure when you are in third grade you can win the golden badge. Is it okay if this year I try for it?'

Kyra nodded and smiled at Tejas.

Maths was to me what reading was to Kyra. Tejas and I were sure that when she would be in third grade no one would be able to stop her from winning the golden badge.

'But what about Annika, my best friend Ambi's sister? She is a third grader and she reads a lot. I bet it would be hard to beat her!' Kyra said.

Tejas suddenly turned pale and chewed on his lucky pencil. I knew that Tejas didn't like chewing on his favourite pencil. So I was certain he was nervous. And I felt pretty sure it was the name Annika that was making him nervous.

The bus stopped and we all got off.

'We'll meet up for football in the evening,' I called out to Tejas but he was walking far in front of me and didn't turn around to answer.

Why Me?

'Mom ... Mom ... Arjun will have a reading competition in school!' Kyra screamed so loudly that even Rio who stayed next door would have heard.

'That's great, Arjun,' Mom said.

'And Mom, if their class wins, they'll have a night stay in school and get to see through a telescope! How lucky these third graders are!' Besides being a drama queen and a complaint box, Kyra was a chatterbox too.

'That sounds nice, but Arjun can't go for a night stay.'

'Why?' I asked, startled. Not that I was going to help in reading, but if we did win, the night stay with the telescope would be one of the world's best things!

'The last time you went to Tejas's house for a night stay, you broke your foot, and before that when you went to Nani's house, you broke your arm and made her break her foot!'

'But it wasn't my mistake! I fell from the front steps at Tejas's house and at Nani's house she tried to put some smelly oil on my hair. That's when we both fell from the bed.' I managed to justify both my falls. 'The night stay in school would be so much fun, I would get to see through a telescope!'

'No, Arjun. It's a complete no!' Mom said firmly.

'But Mom, the best reader will get a golden badge!' Kyra announced. What a pain sisters can be.

'A golden badge! But Arjun, you don't even try to read. Your dad has bought you so many books. Kyra reads them all. If you tried, maybe you could move from a Snail reader to a Bull reader.'

'But Mom, we were talking about the night stay. Why are you talking about Snails and Bulls?'

'It's a NO. I don't want anyone getting another broken leg.'

Mom being an accountant always took Maths into account and came to conclusions about possible future events. But you can't use Maths in everything!

'Could *I* go instead?' Kyra jumped in.

This time I really got angry. Non-violence was not going to work here.

'It's not for your class!' I shook her.

Kyra pouted and began whining.

'Drama queen,' I murmured.

'Arjun called me a drama queen in school too.' Her wailing was turning into howling.

'Arjun, can you be nice to your little sister?' Mom asked, trying to console Kyra.

'She is a little monster,' I said, still angry with Mom for not giving me permission for the night stay.

'Am not.'

'You are.'

'Am not.'

'Are.'

We carried on back and forth like this till Mom screamed, 'Will you both stop!'

'Now say sorry to your sister.'

'Why should I say sorry to her?'

I wondered how Gandhiji managed to stay calm! Maybe he didn't have a monstrous sister like Kyra.

I walked off to my room, which I unfortunately shared with Kyra.

Her part of the room was a dazzling pink, stacked with books, and Dad had helped Kyra paint her wall with butterflies.

My part of the room was a glamorous green, with cool rackets and tiny airplanes. Dad had helped me paint my wall with numbers. Mom had got me a numbered bedspread and a pencil stand with my lucky number 10.

Since it was Friday, I pulled out my no. 5 jersey from my cupboard. All my clothes had numbers according to the days of the week. I ran to the park to play with Tejas. The evenings were of course much cooler than the daytime.

But Tejas was not there, so I joined Rio and Rehan.

Rio was a great shot. 'Where did you learn to shoot so well, Rio?' I asked.

'*I born in Brazil, Arjun, so I kick ball well,*' Rio said in her bad English.

'*I like Brazil, my name also from city in Brazil called Rio de Janeiro, my elder brother name Paris,*

he born there, and my younger brother name India he born here.'

I imagined myself being named North Pole and Kyra South Pole.

I wondered why Tejas hadn't come to play.

When I called his house, no one had answered.

So I spent the weekend playing each and every video game I had with Rehan, the distracted kid, who was not distracted when he played video games.

Count Begins

On Monday morning when I saw Tejas's name on the white tally paper Ms Books had hung in the class and labelled "The Read Drive", I knew exactly what Tejas was doing during the weekend.

He had been busy reading in the secret treehouse in his backyard. I bet he must have even put up a "Do Not Disturb – Reading in Progress" board.

Sometimes he can be a big bore.

I was surprised to see Tejas had seven books to his name.

Sheen - Six!

Rio - Three!

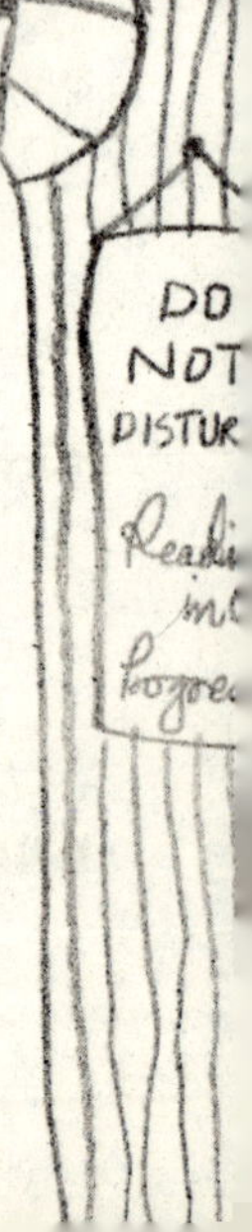

Everyone in the class had a number in front of their names except Rehan and me. In total the class had read 41 books. Even the Snail readers had contributed!

Wow! Maybe we could win this competition and win the night-stay-telescope-viewing award, after all! I felt really excited about the night stay and at the same time was worried that Mom would definitely not allow me.

On Tuesday the total went up to 53 books and Tejas now had nine books to his name. Sheen was one book behind him.

On Wednesday, the total was 67, and Tejas now had 12 books to his name. Sheen was still one book behind him, at second place.

'Arjun, when will you contribute for the *Read Drive*?' Sheen asked me.

I glared at her.

'Maybe once the *Read Drive* is over!' she answered, instead of waiting for me to say something.

What an unkind girl!

During break time, I found Tejas reading in the

playground. 'It's not so sunny today. We can take turns at the swing. Are you going to read all day?' I asked, irritated.

He didn't answer.

'Why are you being such a reading wizard?'

'Aren't you a Maths wizard?' he asked, looking up from his book.

'But you can't hate Maths,' I said.

'You can't hate reading as well. There is so much to know and learn,' Tejas argued back.

'But the world is all done up mathematically. It's round and it's divided proportionately into land and water. The planets are all positioned mathematically and ...'

'But if you hadn't read all of this, how would you have known that?' I had to admit, Tejas's question stumped me.

'But ...' the bell rang and we had to get back to our class.

It was time for Maths and I couldn't wait to see what we would learn today.

In Maths class, I looked over at Tejas. He was busy reading a book on his lap and not concentrating on fractions.

Even Sheen had a book on her lap! These people had to be crazy to read during the most interesting class of the day.

On Thursday, the class total went up to 79, and Tejas's was 15. We were sure to win the competition. I was really proud of the way Tejas had been reading so much, though I had been missing him terribly at playtime. At the rate Tejas was going, he would beat everyone.

My only concern now was Mom. But I couldn't think of anything to convince her.

During break time Tejas was reading *The Weird School.*

'You haven't read a single book,' Tejas told me.

'Do I ask you why you don't pay attention in Maths class?' I asked him, getting angry.

'But Maths and reading are two different things and it's impossible to not like reading.'

'It's impossible to not like Maths!' I claimed.

'But don't you understand? If everyone is not going to contribute, we will not win, and then there will be no night stay or seeing through the telescope!' Tejas said in one breath.

'But you are reading and so is the rest of the class, so we *could* win this,' I insisted.

'Uhh ... have you forgotten about the Cheetah reader Annika in 3B? You were the one who told me about her! I am sure she has read more books than me, and the their class's total must be much higher than ours as they have more Cheetah readers, you fool! Don't you remember you had done the calculation?' Tejas asked in one breath.

Oh no! How could I forget they had more Cheetah readers than us! And mathematically, the more the number of Cheetah readers, the more would be the number of books in the kitty. And of course, *Annika*! How could I forget her!

'3B wants to win just as much as we do!' Tejas said. When Tejas gave such logical reasoning to me, it started sounding like Maths.

'But maybe if we all try ...' Tejas began. By all, he meant Rehan and me, of course. 'Then we could at least win the night stay, if not the golden badge,' Tejas said, trying to inspire me.

That's what I liked about Tejas. He was not only thinking about winning the golden badge himself but about the whole class, and that is why he's my best friend.

'By how many books is Annika ahead of you? And is their class total higher than ours?' I asked, getting worried.

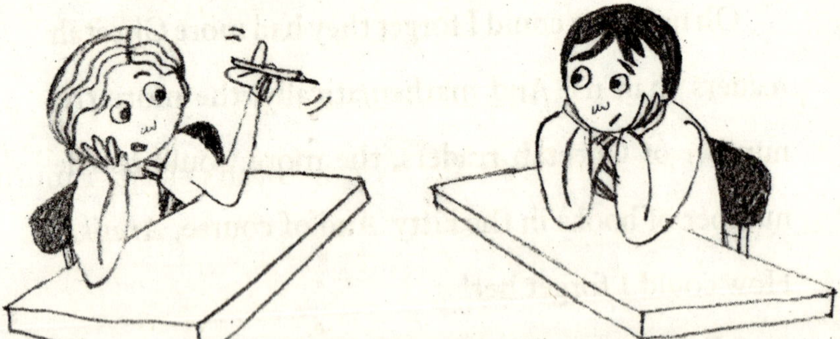

Seeing the total on the sheet Ms Books had hung on the board and the way Tejas was reading, I had assumed we were surely going to win the *Read Drive*.

But now Tejas had got me thinking. I had to be a fool to forget about Annika and 3B's other Cheetah readers.

'I don't know,' Tejas said doubtfully.

'Can't we find out?' I asked.

'No, they are writing the total in their class journal and keeping it a secret till next Friday.' Tejas shook his lucky pencil so hard, I thought it would break.

There had to be a way to find out something!

One Small Lie

All evening I kept wondering how many books 3B had read.

How many books had Annika read?

Were they ahead of us?

The way Tejas was reading, wouldn't he be the one to win the golden badge?

Above all, was our class winning or losing?

And if we won, would Mom let me go for the night stay?

My mind was a pool of questions.

At bedtime, I lay beside Dad while he read to Kyra. He was reading a book on Mahatma Gandhi. 'The famous leader who was unique,' Ms Books had said.

I heard Dad tell Kyra about a skinny-looking man wearing a dhoti, with a stick in his hand, who had helped India get freedom from the British.

This man sounded interesting!

Dad read about Gandhi's struggles, non-violence, his efforts in South Africa and his fasts. People were moved by his speeches, simplicity and truthfulness and agreed to fight the British without violence because of him.

Whoa! This skinny man seemed to be a hero. His non-violence theory really had to be great to be followed by an entire nation.

'We shall complete the rest tomorrow, Kyra.'

'Now it's lights off time,' Dad said.

Awww! I wish he would read the whole thing now. Gandhi was cool!

But the lights went off. Poof! And we fell asleep.

***

'Kyra, could you hurry up? I need to use the bathroom!' I screamed from outside. 'We are going to be late for school!'

'The shower handle is stuck!' she yelled.

'Gosh! Just pull it harder. You can't do anything!' I yelled back.

'Of course I can do everything. I can do everything better than you!' she screamed louder.

But that is when it hit me. Who else in the world would know the answers to my questions except the monster?

Annika's sister, Ambi, and Kyra, were best friends.

'Do you know how many books 3B has read?' I asked as soon as she got out of the bathroom.

'And why should I tell you that?' Kyra asked, arms folded.

'Because I am your brother,' I said with all my brotherly might.

'But you called me a drama queen,' she said, pouting again.

I started getting angry and opened my mouth to tell her that she *was* one of the biggest drama queens I had ever seen and she could surpass any film actor where being dramatic was concerned.

Suddenly I stopped and thought about what Dad had read aloud about Mahatma Gandhi. What would Gandhiji have done in such a situation? Gandhiji hadn't used violence even in his speech and still had got freedom from the British.

So maybe if I was polite, I could get my answers from Kyra too. Now that seemed quite mathematical.

'OK, I am sorry for that,' I said, trying to sound nice.

'See, you made a face again,' Kyra growled.

I gave her a stiff smile. 'Now is this OK? Could you tell me?' I pleaded.

She said reluctantly, 'Well, 3B has read 86 books.'

'Eighty six books already! And Annika?' I asked, trying to remain calm.

After a never-ending pause, Kyra finally said, 'Seventeen.'

Seventeen!

I quickly calculated. Tejas had read 15 books and was two books behind Annika. Our class, 3A, had read 79 books. So 3B was *seven* books ahead of us!

Seven books meant Tejas and all our Cheetah readers would have to increase their reading speed!

But even if we tried, 3B would still be ahead of us as they had more Cheetah readers. And that meant no night stay and no seeing through the telescope! Not that Mom had agreed yet, but at least if we won, I stood a chance.

When I entered the class, I saw the total had gone up to 93. But I couldn't see what use that was. 3B's total must have gone up as high as a skyscraper. And

Tejas's total was 18. I was sure Annika's total was at least 20, maybe more.

I wondered what I could do to help us win this competition.

And then I did something I had never done before or thought of doing.

I picked up a pencil and wrote on the white tally sheet Ms Books had hung, *Mahatma Gandhi – Arjun.*

My hands shook as I wrote it. 'But one small lie wouldn't make so much of a difference,' I thought. *Just one.*

'Good job, Arjun,' Ms Books said. 'I am proud of you. It isn't important to win the competition but it is important to read.'

I felt sick in the stomach, but I reasoned that this was a harmless lie.

Tejas smiled at me and whispered, 'Thanks for contributing.'

I tried to smile.

I wanted to tell Tejas that we were way behind 3B and that he would not be able to win the golden badge unless he gave up eating and sleeping and only read books. But I thought that would make him even more nervous about the competition than he already was.

Part of me wanted to tell my best friend that I hadn't read the book but had listened to my dad reading it. I wanted to admit that I was lying.

But another part of me didn't want Tejas to think I was a liar.

I knew Gandhiji would never have lied. And that is why I was not going to do it again! Only once, that was it! It wouldn't do any harm.

In the library I couldn't complete even one Sudoku. I was getting scared. What if anyone found out that I hadn't read *Gandhi* but had just heard it!

I saw Rehan; he was busy with his toy dinosaur.

I wished he would read instead. But how could I ask Rehan to read when I was not reading?

I saw Ms Books. She was coming towards me. Gosh! Had she found out that I was lying?

'Here, Arjun, I have got you another book for the weekend. Since we have only one more week left, I want you all to read as much as you can. I am sure you will enjoy this one.'

I sighed with relief. She hadn't found out!

This time I didn't tell her that I couldn't read the book. I was scared to speak. I just took the book from her.

Shall I?

Usually weekends were the best part of the week for me, but this one wasn't about to turn out that way.

Rehan came over to play video games. After our eighth game, he said, 'You've lost every single game, Arjun!'

'I don't feel like playing,' I said.

In the evening Rio called up. '*I wait for you at park, you not come for football?*'

'Umm ... I am busy, Rio,' I said and hung up. I just

didn't want to meet anyone. I was terrified they would find out about my lie.

'Hey dude, Ronaldo scored a goal, and you're not cheering?' Dad asked at night when we were watching TV.

I was hardly concentrating on the match.

'Arjun, I have got gulab jamun for you. It's in the fridge and you can have it for dessert,' Mom called out.

'I don't want any.' I quickly ran back to my room. What if Mom and Dad found out my secret?

After lying about having read the book, I just couldn't be myself. I was pretending all the time. I hadn't realised how one stupid lie could change your whole world.

A little later Mom came in. 'Is everything OK with you, Arjun?'

I nodded.

'You don't want gulab jamun today?' she asked, very surprised.

'No Mom.'

'Is something bothering you, dear?' Mom asked, taking my hand in hers.

Yes, I wanted to share my guilt with her. And if I kept it locked in me any further, my heart would explode. I wanted to tell her that I was dying to go for the night stay and see through the telescope. I wanted to tell her how badly I wanted our class to win!

She ruffled my hair with her hands. It felt nice. I was about to confess to her. But ... what if she stopped talking to me for lying? And what if she started hating me? Then she would never let me stay the night at school even if our class won! Which was unlikely anyway because Annika was reading at a speed greater than the Cheetah speed.

She tucked me in bed and kissed me good night. Kyra was fast asleep. She always looks like an angel when she sleeps. After a while, Dad popped in. 'Hey, you still awake, Arjun?'

'I can't sleep,' I murmured.

'Sometimes when I can't sleep, I read. Do you want me to read to you?' Dad asked softly.

'Could you complete the Mahatma Gandhi book for me?' I asked.

'Sure dear,' he whispered, lest Kyra woke up.

I snuggled with Dad and he read to me all about Gandhiji's encounters, his non-cooperation movement, his salt march, his inspiration, King Harishchandra, who held onto the truth even in difficult times, and then an event about how Gandhiji as a kid had once lied to his parents.

His parents were not aware that Gandhiji had lied, but Gandhiji was filled with guilt. He then wrote a letter to his father admitting to him his lie, and promising that he would never ever lie again in his life.

Whoa! Gandhiji had lied! And he had had the courage to admit it to his parents. And also to promise to never ever lie again. He really was a great man and deserved to be called the father of the nation.

One thing was certain. Lying was a difficult thing to do. But to hide the fact that you had lied was even more difficult.

On Sunday morning, there came a loud crash. I ran down to see what it was.

Kyra had broken Mom's favourite cookie jar! She looked super scared. I wondered if she was going to run away.

'What happened?' Mom came running out from her room.

'I ... I broke your favourite cookie jar,' she said, and burst out crying.

This was no ordinary cookie jar. Mom had had it since she was a kid. It was Nani's special gift to her. Mom was quiet, so were we.

I waited for Mom to explode ...

I waited for Kyra to howl and then get grounded for the whole of next week. That should have been the logical order of things.

'I am sorry, I shall be more careful next time,' Kyra said, tears still running down her cheeks.

'It's OK, Kyra, I am glad you owned up and didn't try to hide or run away,' Mom said quietly.

Bingo! She wasn't angry! No grounding! No calculation this time!

Mom added, 'As for the jar, yes, it was precious, but we can try to fix it.'

'Can I help you fix it up?' Kyra asked.

'Sure, we can do it together,' Mom said with the hint of a smile.

Mom hadn't gotten angry with Kyra even after she had broken her favourite jar, and the only explanation for that could be that she had owned up to it!

Gandhiji, the father of the nation, had had the courage to apologise for his mistake. My little sister, a monster, a drama queen and a chatterbox had had the courage to do the same.

'What about me?' I asked myself.

'If they could do it, why couldn't I?'

Read Read Read!!!

Before another thought crossed my mind, I went to Mom. 'I want to share something with you!' I said, looking at the floor.

'Come here, dear.' She made me sit on her lap, facing her.

My heart was beating like I had just run a marathon. Kyra was there too, playing with her dolls. I wondered what she would think of me.

I was choking with emotion but I knew I had to confess. The burden of my falsehood was suffocating

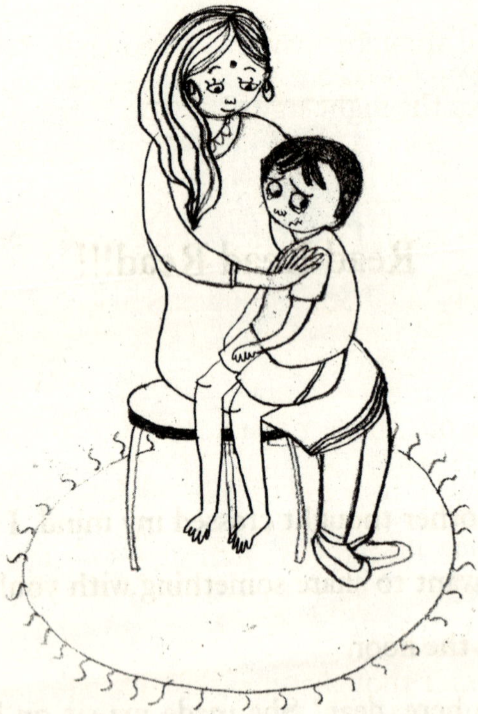

me. Even Gandhiji had confessed to his parents about his lie. I opened and closed my mouth a couple of times and then took a deep breath. Then I finally said it. 'I ... I lied.' My eyes filled with tears.

'I lied that I read a book for the Read Drive but I didn't,' I said very softly.

'I lied because I wanted my class to win the *Read Drive*, and thought maybe ... just maybe you would send me for the night stay if we won.' I felt my cheeks turn hot.

'I am s-sorry. I shall never repeat this again.' My voice shook, but I felt a hundred kilograms had been lifted off my heart.

I spoke out the last thing that was troubling me. 'Are you and Dad going to hate me for this?' I asked. I gave a quick look at Kyra to find out if she hated me already.

Mom said thoughtfully, 'We all make mistakes, Arjun, but many people do not have the courage to own up to them. I am very proud that you have spoken the truth. But I wish you had not lied in the first place. As for Dad and me hating you, we could never do that. We love you for what you are.'

'How can I get myself out of this mess? Would you help me?' I asked, feeling much better.

'Yes, Arjun, you can fix this up by reading the same book that you lied about, and then count it for the *Read Drive*, and also by never lying again.' She gave me her warmest hug and I knew she wouldn't hate me.

'I'll never lie again, Mom, I promise,' I said, squeezing her with all my might.

With Mom's help I could fix anything!

Kyra smiled from the corner of her mouth and I knew even she didn't hate me.

I spent the entire Sunday reading *Gandhi*. I looked up the meanings of the words I didn't understand. It was not an easy read for a Snail reader, but I enjoyed it.

I also discovered that I liked reading about Gandhi's life. He was a real guy, not a made-up one.

The book was not scary.

It was not girly.

It was not boring.

It was not kiddish.

It didn't make me feel sad.

As a matter of fact, it made me feel good.

Next day in school I erased my name from the sheet Ms Books had hung, and rewrote my name proudly, in the best cursive handwriting this time. *Mahatma Gandhi - Arjun.*

Tejas frowned. 'You read the same book twice! Are you crazy?'

I smiled at him.

After school I ran to Kyra's class to quickly get 3B's total from her.

'So?' I asked.

'So?' she said.

'OK! So what's their total?' I asked, sighing.

'3B has read 125 books till this morning, and Annika has read 27.'

I felt dizzy. Their Cheetah readers really were running like cheetahs!

Just like the *Read Drive* was important to us, it seemed important to them too, and I think they had given up on sleeping, eating, playing video games and everything else in the world to win this competition.

Rio called up in the evening. '*Hey, Arjun, no play in park?*'

'Sorry Rio, I think I'll read. The *Read Drive* ends on Friday and I really want our class to win,' I said.

'*OK, I read too,*' she said in her broken English and hung up.

Rehan came to play video games. I got tempted, but surprised myself by saying, 'Sorry Rehan, I would rather read today and help our class win.'

He was stunned. 'You reading?'

I nodded, 'Why don't you try too?'

'Not me,' he said.

I took out an easy reader dinosaur book from Kyra's shelf. 'Try this.'

'Dinosaurs?'

I smiled. 'Yes, try it—maybe you will like it!'

He took it with him.

I took out a book for myself. I was going to read *Barack Obama* today. He was the first black president of America. Now that was something cool!

On Tuesday our total was 136, 3B's was 140.

Tejas's score was 29.

Annika's was 30.

Sheen was close to Tejas, and guess what, Rehan had a score of one.

I gave more dinosaur books to Rehan.

And I managed to read *Albert Einstein.* It felt great to read about a mathematician.

On Wednesday, our total was 156.

3B's was 159.

Tejas had scored 33.

Annika had also read 33 books.

By now Rehan had three books to his name.

I read *Pele,* about the great footballer, and *Helen Keller,* about the lady who was blind and deaf but was still an author, a lecturer and an activist.

Wow! We've had some great people on Earth.

On Thursday our total reached 178.

3B's score was 180.

Tejas's was 36.

Annika had read 36 books as well.

Everybody in class was contributing—Rio, Sheen, Rehan and all the others. Even the Snail readers were giving their best.

'Can we have more reading time today, Ms Books, instead of doing Maths?' I asked on Thursday.

Tejas looked surprised.

'Yes Arjun, I am very glad that you have developed your interest in reading. I think we could go one day without Maths.'

'Thank you, Ms Books,' I said, thrilled.

Everyone in class clapped for not having to do Maths today and having more time for reading.

I had never seen Tejas so happy as today. OK, Maths was still my favourite, but today I had to finish *Kalpana Chawla* and *Jawaharlal Nehru.*

On Thursday I read and read and read. I read while having dinner, I read in the bathroom, I read after lights off time with my torch and I read till I fell asleep. Mom didn't stop me.

On Friday morning I skipped taking a shower and finished reading *Ram, the Prince of Ayodhya,*

and on the way to school in the bus I started reading *Mother Teresa.* I finished it while walking to class.

Everyone wrote down the names of the books that they had read. And then Ms Books took the sheet and went to the principal's office with it.

The Results!

After lunch both 3A and 3B gathered in the Arts and Culture Centre of the school with our principal, Mr Gupta, Ms Books and 3B's teacher. It was time to find out who gets to go for the night stay and see through the telescope.

My heart was beating like the drums in a big march past parade.

Tejas was shaking his lucky pencil vigorously.

Rio, Rehan and Sheen stood quietly.

'I am proud of both 3A and 3B for completing the

Read Drive and reading so many books,' Mr Gupta said. He was wearing the red and white *Cat in the Hat* hat of Dr Suess.

'It is not important who wins or loses but the aim of the *Read Drive* was to discover reading. As Dr Suess says, "The more you read, the more you'll learn, and the more you'll learn, the more places you'll go.'

Mr Gupta always said things about Dr Suess.

'Your teachers have told me that even reluctant Snail readers have begun to read books, and soon they will be Bull readers,' he said proudly.

I stole a glance at Ms Books and at Rehan.

'OK, now for the results.' As his voice grew louder, my heart started thumping. I crossed my fingers, and even my toes. Tejas was shaking his pencil like crazy. If there was a better word than crazy to describe his nervousness, I would have used it here, but at this time I couldn't think of anything else except CRAZY! And I knew this because I felt I was going to go crazy if Mr Gupta didn't announce the results soon!

'Well ... the winner for the *Read Drive* is 3 ... B and A! Both the sections have read an equal number of books—198 books each. Which is a lot of books!'

'Yippee!'

'Yeah!'

'Both the classes get to stay in school for the night and see through the telescope!' Mr Gupta announced into the microphone.

Everyone was hooting so loudly that Mr Gupta had to shout out the next announcement. 'And now for the Golden Badge. It was a tough competition and the winner has won by one book. It is Tejas from *3A*!'

Tejas froze. He was in shock and didn't know how to react. Rehan, Rio and I were cheering loudly, 'Yeah! Yeah! Yipee! Whoa!'

Annika did look disappointed but I am sure she was happy because her class had won too!

Mr Gupta gave Tejas the Golden Badge award and I clapped so hard that my hands turned red.

'Since both the classes have won, I shall see all of you tomorrow with your sleeping bags. Your class teachers shall speak to your parents,' Mr Gupta made his final announcement.

On the bus, Kyra kept saying, 'How lucky!' But I wasn't sure how lucky I was. Mom had still not said anything about the night stay.

Chances of Mom allowing me to participate were a mere 2/10 and after knowing that I had lied, it must have come down to 0/10.

'Mom, both the classes have tied for the *Read Drive* and Tejas won the golden badge!' Kyra announced as soon as we reached home.

After lying at school, I felt I didn't deserve the night stay. It was really stupid of me to think that by lying we could win the *Read Drive*.

'Arjun, Ms Books called and she said she was very proud of you and that you had discovered what kind of books you like and also how you helped Rehan to read. I was wondering if you would like to participate in the night stay,' Mom remarked.

'Of course, Mom,' Kyra screamed. 'And if he doesn't want to go, can I go in his place?'

I stared at her.

'I was just asking,' Kyra said.

'May I?' I asked softly.

'Yes, Arjun,' Mom said. 'Since you've owned up about your mistake and you have promised me not to lie again, and also you have developed your reading skills.'

She hugged me.

'Ms Books also says now you are eligible to proceed to the Bull readers' group,' Mom said, sounding pleased.

I jumped on Mom and nearly toppled her off the chair.

'Thanks Mom! You are the best Mumma in the world!' I gave her a tight squishing hug!

I packed my sleeping bag and stuffed whatever I could in my backpack. This was going to be one of the most exciting weekends ever!

About the Author

Arti Sonthalia's first children's book *Big Bully And M-me* was nominated for the Crystal Kite Asia Awards. She also writes for the *Chicken Soup for the Soul,* and when she is not writing she loves listening to soulful music.

OTHER BOOKS YOU MAY LIKE

Bookasura

THE ADVENTURES OF BALA AND THE BOOK-EATING MONSTER

Arundhati Venkatesh

Illustrations: Priya Kuriyan

A strange many-headed creature, Bookasura, makes an appearance when Bala is at his grandparents' house. Bala keeps Bookasura at bay by supplying him with a steady stream of books. But Bala will soon run out of books. What then? Will Bookasura eat Bala up? Or will Bala be able to save himself?

ISBN: 9789351037064
Pages: 64

Koobandhee

THE ADVENTURES OF BALA AND THE BOOK-BARFING MONSTER

Arundhati Venkatesh

Illustrations: Priya Kuriyan

Bala's books—and his life—are under threat. Things get worse when Bala encounters the one-eyed bookbarfing monster, Koobandhee. Will Bala survive? Or will he vanish without a trace? The second story in the award-winning the Book-Asuras series.

ISBN: 9789351039877
Pages: 148

Adventure on Wheels

Prashant Pinge

Illustrations: Priya Kuriyan

Two thieves. Three orphan kids. An accidental kidnapping. A failed attempted robbery. It's one hell of an adventure on wheels, which at times has you rolling on the floor with laughter and also wiping a tear or two. A heart-warming tale of fun and adventure.

ISBN: 9789351039877
Pages: 148

The Adventures of Mooli and The Blue-Legged Alien

Asha Nehemiah

Illustrations: Tanaya Vyas

Mooli's meddling ways usually get him into trouble but he also has some of the best ideas. Soups loves reading and is super-smart. Join them on some awesome adventures as they try out tricks and stunts which no one has ever thought of before!

ISBN: 9789352750689
Pages: 72

Book Uncle and Me
Uma Krishnaswami

This innovative novel is a celebration of literacy and the power of books, and of the actions of a single young character within a larger community. It is written in lineated prose, for 7-9 year olds.

ISBN: 9788184778502
Pages: 108

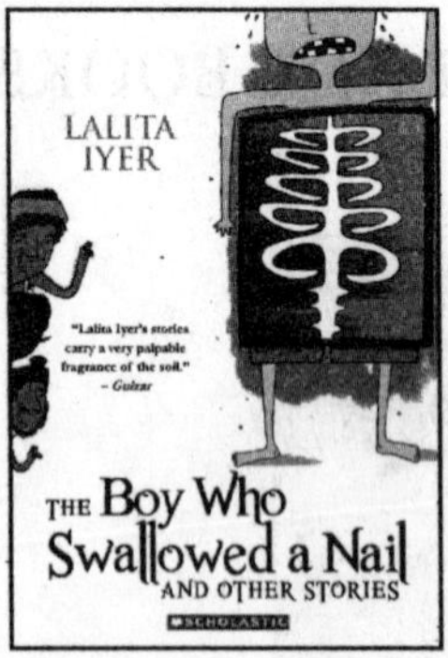

The Boy Who Swallowed a Nail and Other Stories
Lalita Iyer
Illustrations: Shamika Kocharekar

Lalita Iyer's family is always up to something. Read about their quirks and adventures in this charming collection of stories.

ISBN: 9789385887260
Pages: 72

The Great River Magic
Nandini Nayar
Illustrations: Lavanya Karthik

Join Sangeeta, Neeta and Dutta on a magical quest that teaches them to cherish the magic in the world around them. A lip-smacking, racy, environmental adventure!

ISBN. 9789386106483
Pages: 96

The Star that Saved the Day
Nalini Sorensen
Illustrations: Shreya Sen

Yohan and Yash's mom reads her horoscope every single day. But one day, the newspaper carries a horoscope like none she has ever read before. Read this simple and funny story to find out how a star saved the day!

ISBN: 9789386106421
Pages: 64